HICKORY PUBLIC LIBRARY

3 2509 11229 14 9

W9-CPK-366

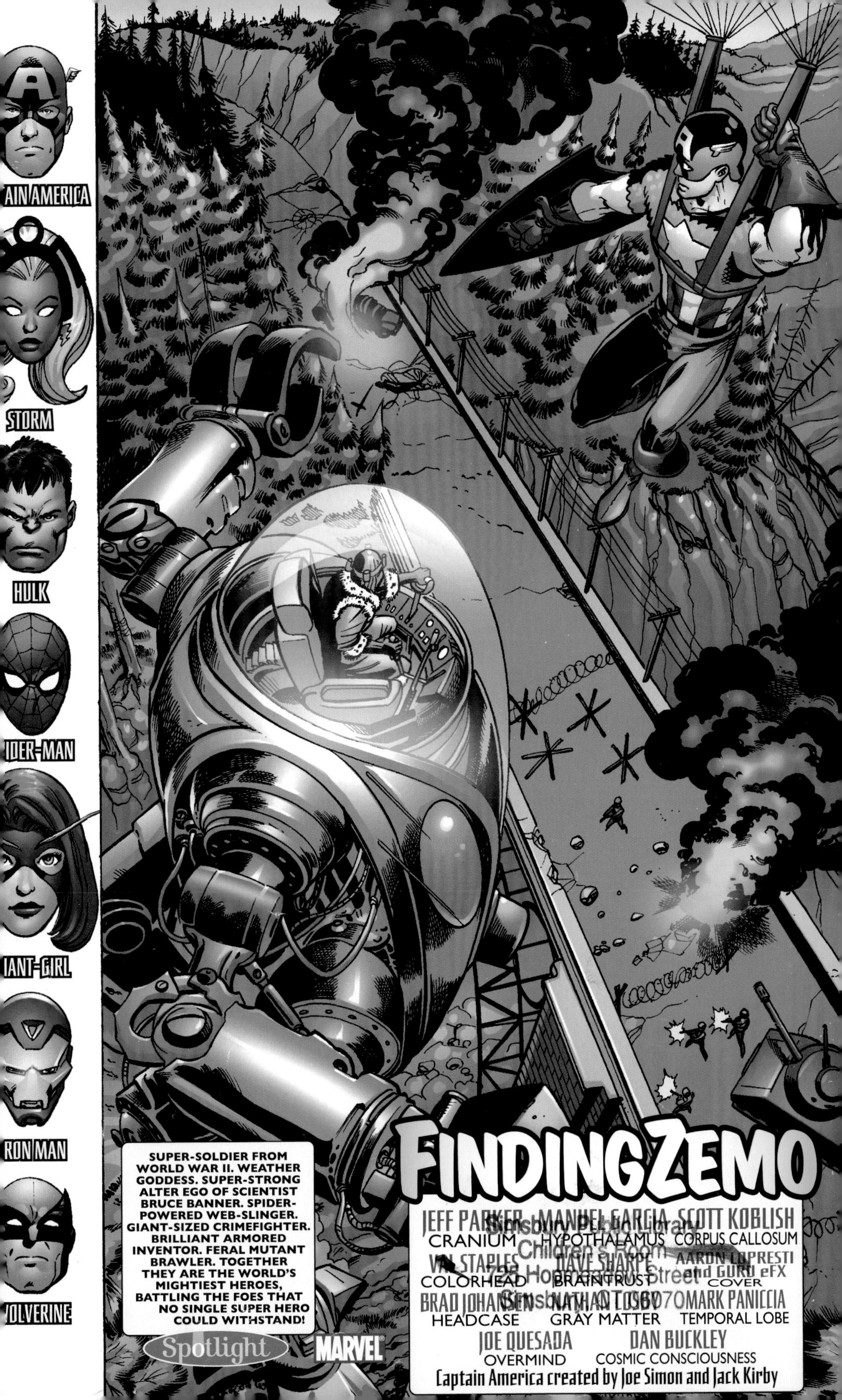

AIN AMERICA
STORM
HULK
IDER-MAN
IANT-GIRL
RON MAN
OLVERINE
SUPER-SOLDIER FROM WORLD WAR II. WEATHER GODDESS. SUPER-STRONG ALTER EGO OF SCIENTIST BRUCE BANNER. SPIDER-POWERED WEB-SLINGER. GIANT-SIZED CRIMEFIGHTER. BRILLIANT ARMORED INVENTOR. FERAL MUTANT BRAWLER. TOGETHER THEY ARE THE WORLD'S MIGHTIEST HEROES, BATTLING THE FOES THAT NO SINGLE SUPER HERO COULD WITHSTAND!
Spotlight
MARVEL
FINDING ZEMO
JEFF PARKER CRANIUM
MANUEL GARCIA HYPOTHALAMUS
SCOTT KOBLISH CORPUS CALLOSUM
VAL STAPLES COLORHEAD
DAVE SHARPE BRAINTRUST
AARON LOPRESTI and GURU eFX COVER
BRAD JOHANSEN HEADCASE
NATHAN COSBY GRAY MATTER
MARK PANICCIA TEMPORAL LOBE
JOE QUESADA OVERMIND
DAN BUCKLEY COSMIC CONSCIOUSNESS
Captain America created by Joe Simon and Jack Kirby

VISIT US AT
www.abdopublishing.com

Reinforced library bound edition published in 2008 by Spotlight, a division of the ABDO Publishing Group, 8000 West 78th Street, Edina, Minnesota 55439. Spotlight produces high-quality reinforced library bound editions for schools and libraries. Published by agreement with Marvel Characters, Inc.

MARVEL, and all related character names and the distinctive likenesses thereof are trademarks of Marvel Characters, Inc., and is/are used with permission. Copyright © 2007 Marvel Characters, Inc. All rights reserved. www.marvel.com

MARVEL, Avengers: TM & © 2007 Marvel Characters, Inc. All rights reserved. www.marvel.com. This book is produced under license from Marvel Characters, Inc.

Library of Congress Cataloging-in-Publication Data

Parker, Jeff, 1966-
  Finding Zemo / Jeff Parker, cranium ; Manuel Garcia, hypothalamus ; Scott Koblish, corpus callosum ; Val Staples, colorhead ; Dave Sharpe, braintrust ; Aaron Lopresti and GURU eFX, cover. - Reinforced library bound ed.
     p. cm. -- (The Avengers)
  "Marvel age"--Cover.
  Revision of issue 3 of Marvel adventures, the Avengers.
  ISBN 978-1-59961-383-3
  1. Graphic novels. I. Garcia, Manuel. II. Marvel adventures, the Avengers. 3. III. Title.

PN6728.A94P33 2008
741.5'973--dc22

                                                    2007020254

All Spotlight books have reinforced library bindings and are manufactured in the United States of America.

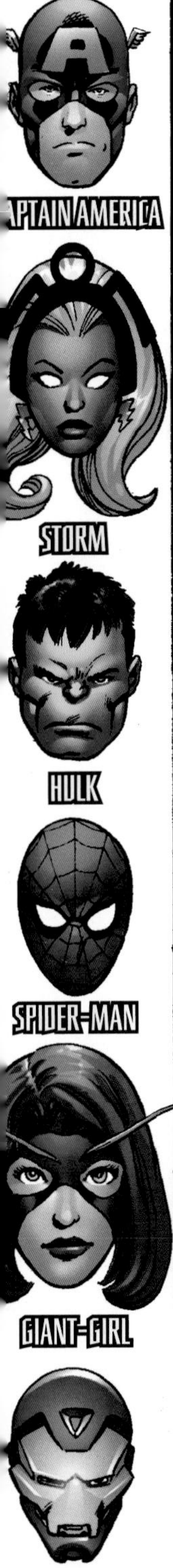
PTAIN AMERICA
STORM
HULK
SPIDER-MAN
GIANT-GIRL
IRON MAN
WOLVERINE

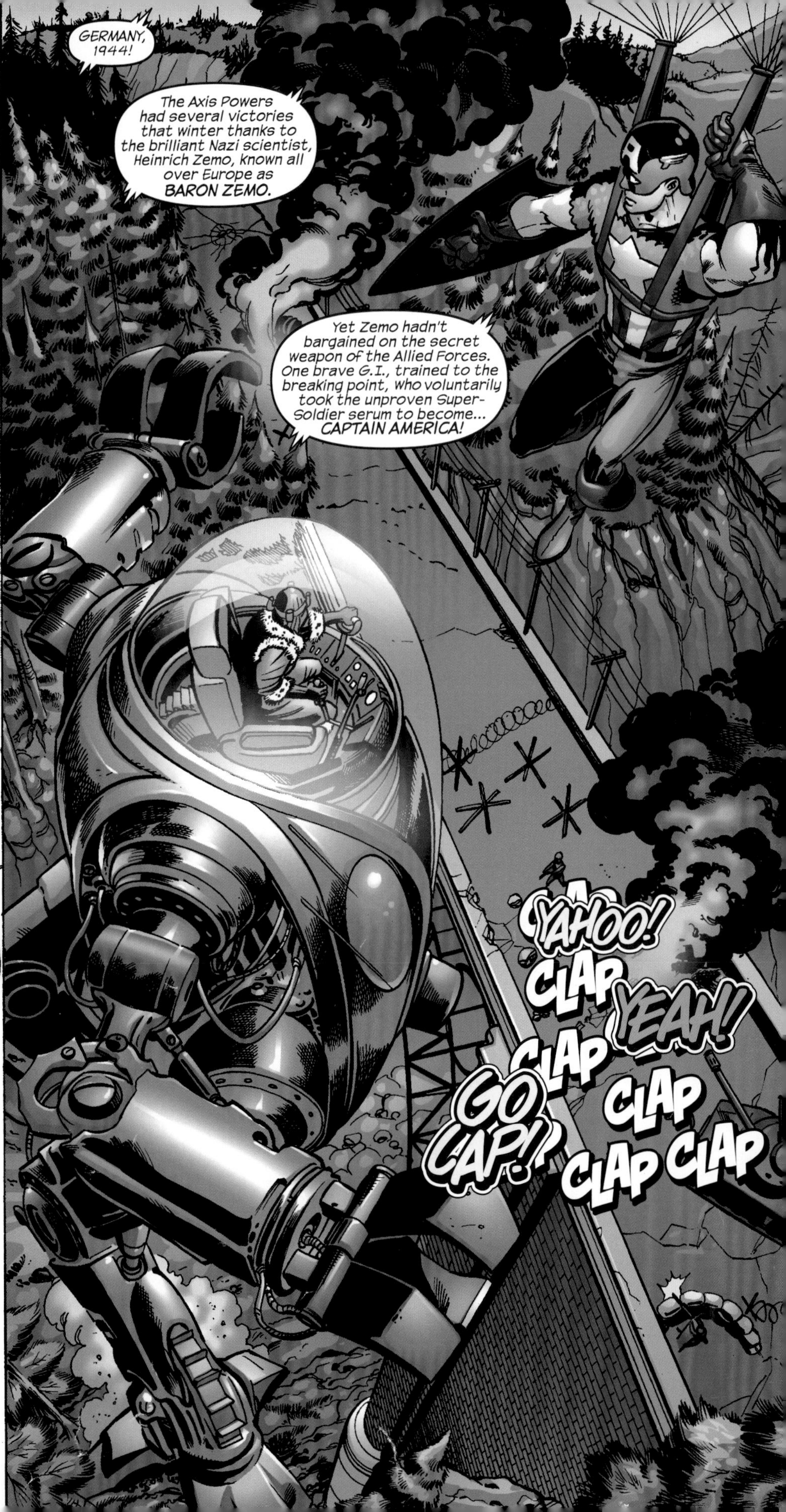
GERMANY, 1944!
The Axis Powers had several victories that winter thanks to the brilliant Nazi scientist, Heinrich Zemo, known all over Europe as BARON ZEMO.
Yet Zemo hadn't bargained on the secret weapon of the Allied Forces. One brave G.I., trained to the breaking point, who voluntarily took the unproven Super-Soldier serum to become... CAPTAIN AMERICA!
YAHOO!
CLAP
YEAH!
CLAP
GO CAP!!
CLAP
CLAP CLAP

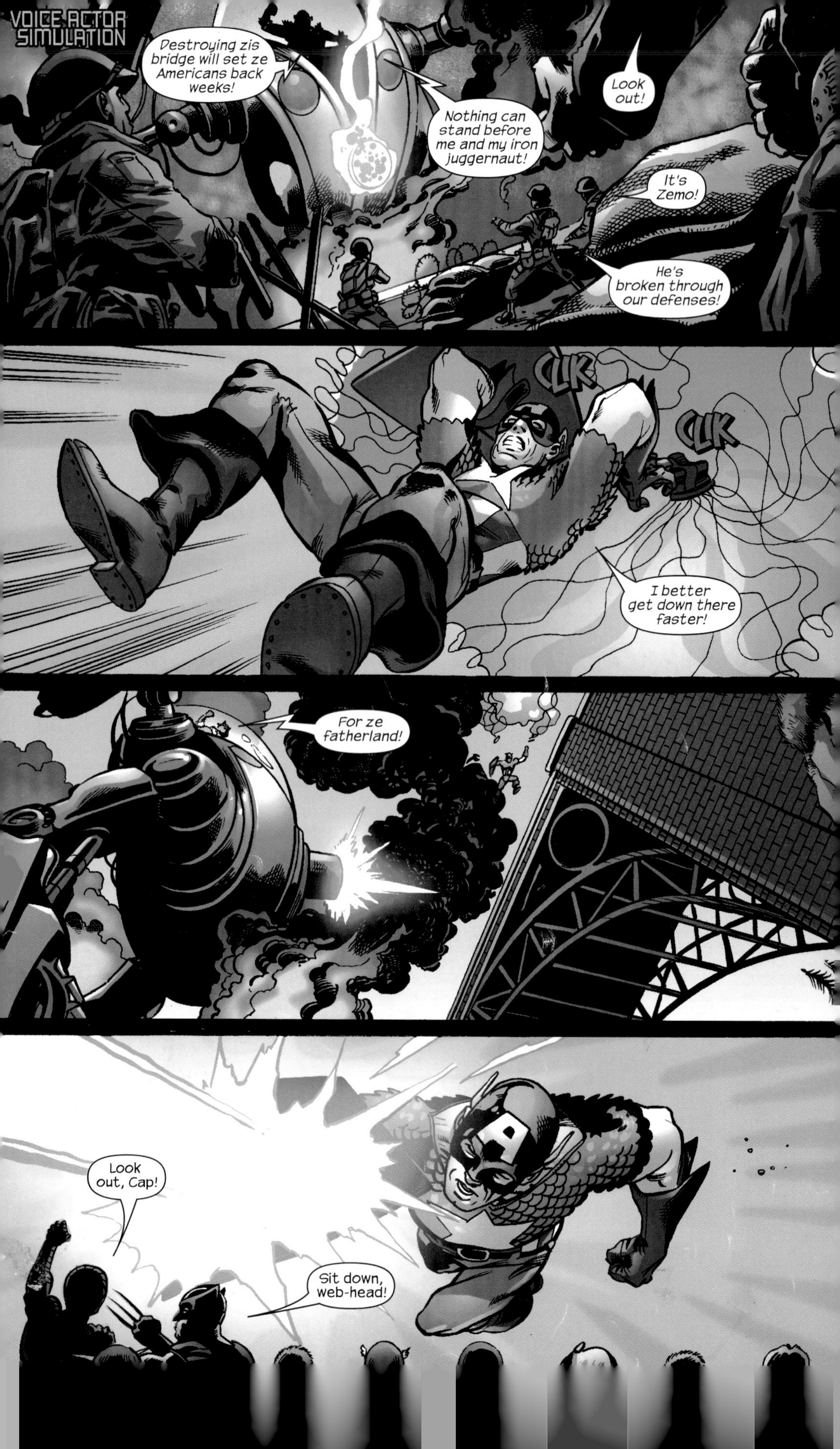
VOICE ACTOR SIMULATION
Destroying zis bridge will set ze Americans back weeks!
Nothing can stand before me and my iron juggernaut!
Look out!
It's Zemo!
He's broken through our defenses!
CLIK
CLIK
I better get down there faster!
For ze fatherland!
Look out, Cap!
Sit down, web-head!

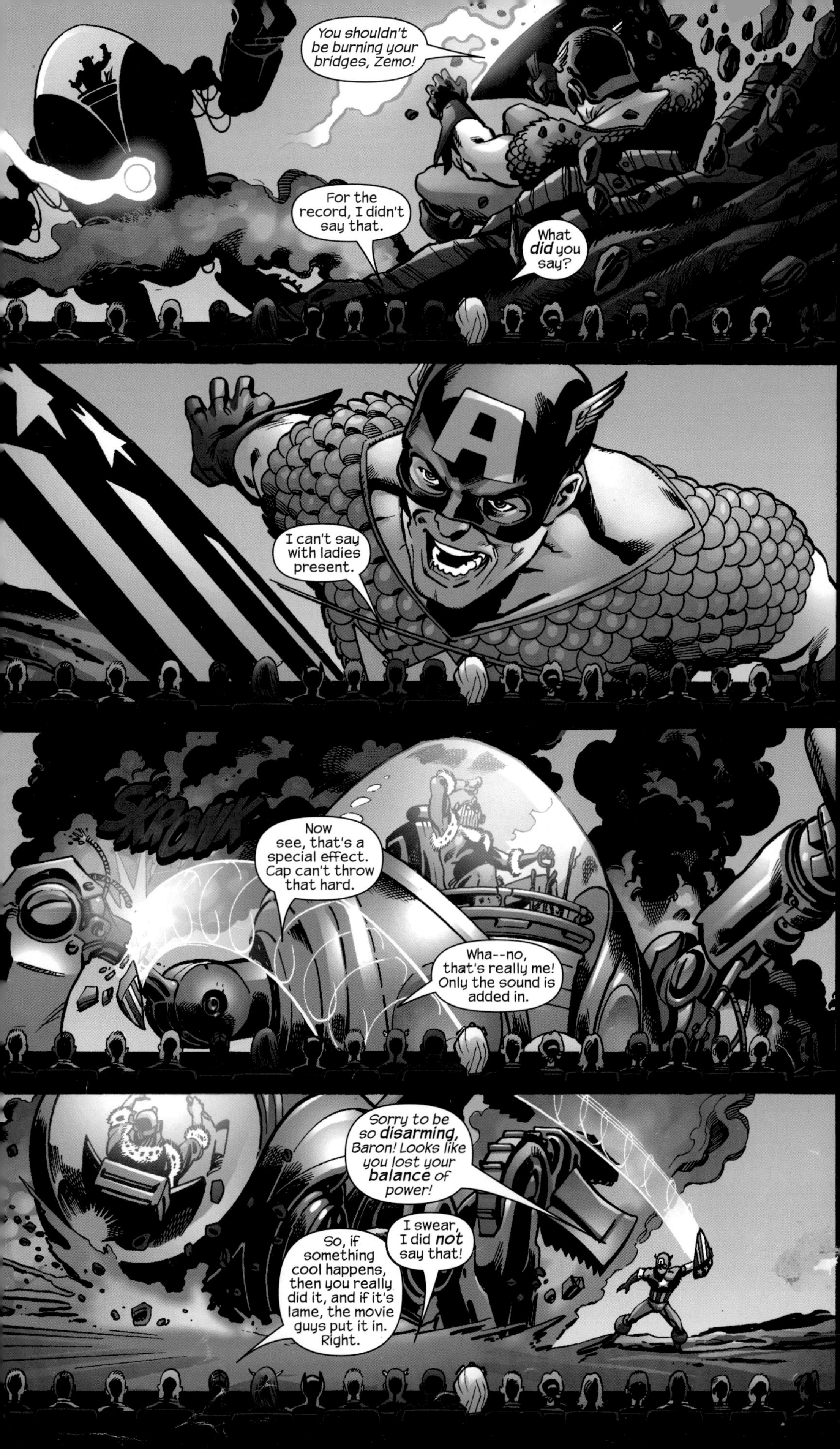

You shouldn't be burning your bridges, Zemo!
For the record, I didn't say that.
What **did** you say?
I can't say with ladies present.
Now see, that's a special effect. Cap can't throw that hard.
Wha--no, that's really me! Only the sound is added in.
Sorry to be so **disarming,** Baron! Looks like you lost your **balance** of power!
I swear, I did **not** say that!
So, if something cool happens, then you really did it, and if it's lame, the movie guys put it in. Right.

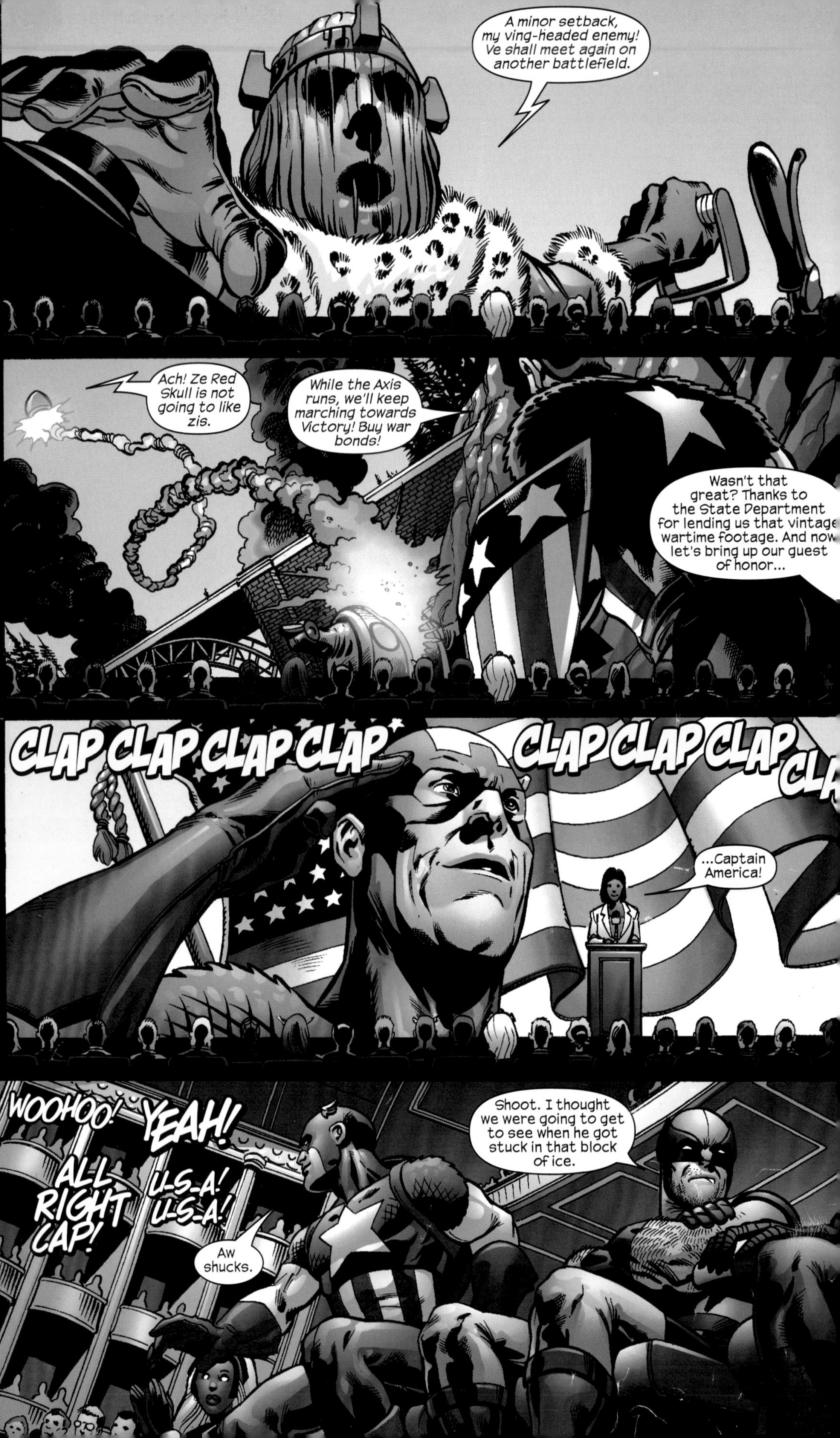

A minor setback, my ving-headed enemy! Ve shall meet again on another battlefield.
Ach! Ze Red Skull is not going to like zis.
While the Axis runs, we'll keep marching towards Victory! Buy war bonds!
Wasn't that great? Thanks to the State Department for lending us that vintage wartime footage. And now let's bring up our guest of honor...
CLAP CLAP CLAP CLAP
CLAP CLAP CLAP
...Captain America!
WOOHOO! YEAH!
ALL RIGHT CAP!
U-S-A! U-S-A!
Aw shucks.
Shoot. I thought we were going to get to see when he got stuck in that block of ice.

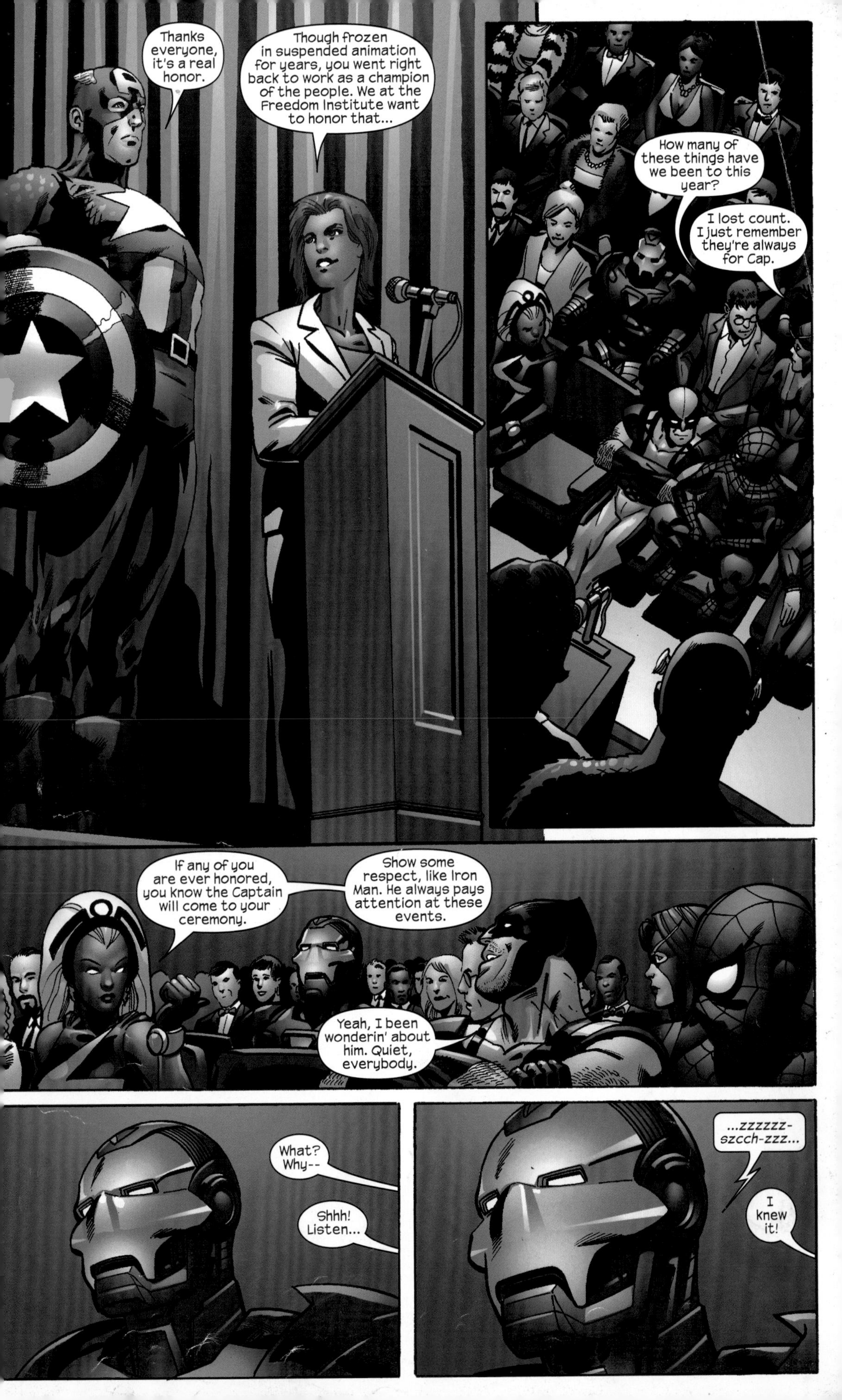
Thanks everyone, it's a real honor.
Though frozen in suspended animation for years, you went right back to work as a champion of the people. We at the Freedom Institute want to honor that...
How many of these things have we been to this year?
I lost count. I just remember they're always for Cap.
If any of you are ever honored, you know the Captain will come to your ceremony.
Show some respect, like Iron Man. He always pays attention at these events.
Yeah, I been wonderin' about him. Quiet, everybody.
What? Why--
Shhh! Listen...
...zzzzzz-szcch-zzz...
I knew it!

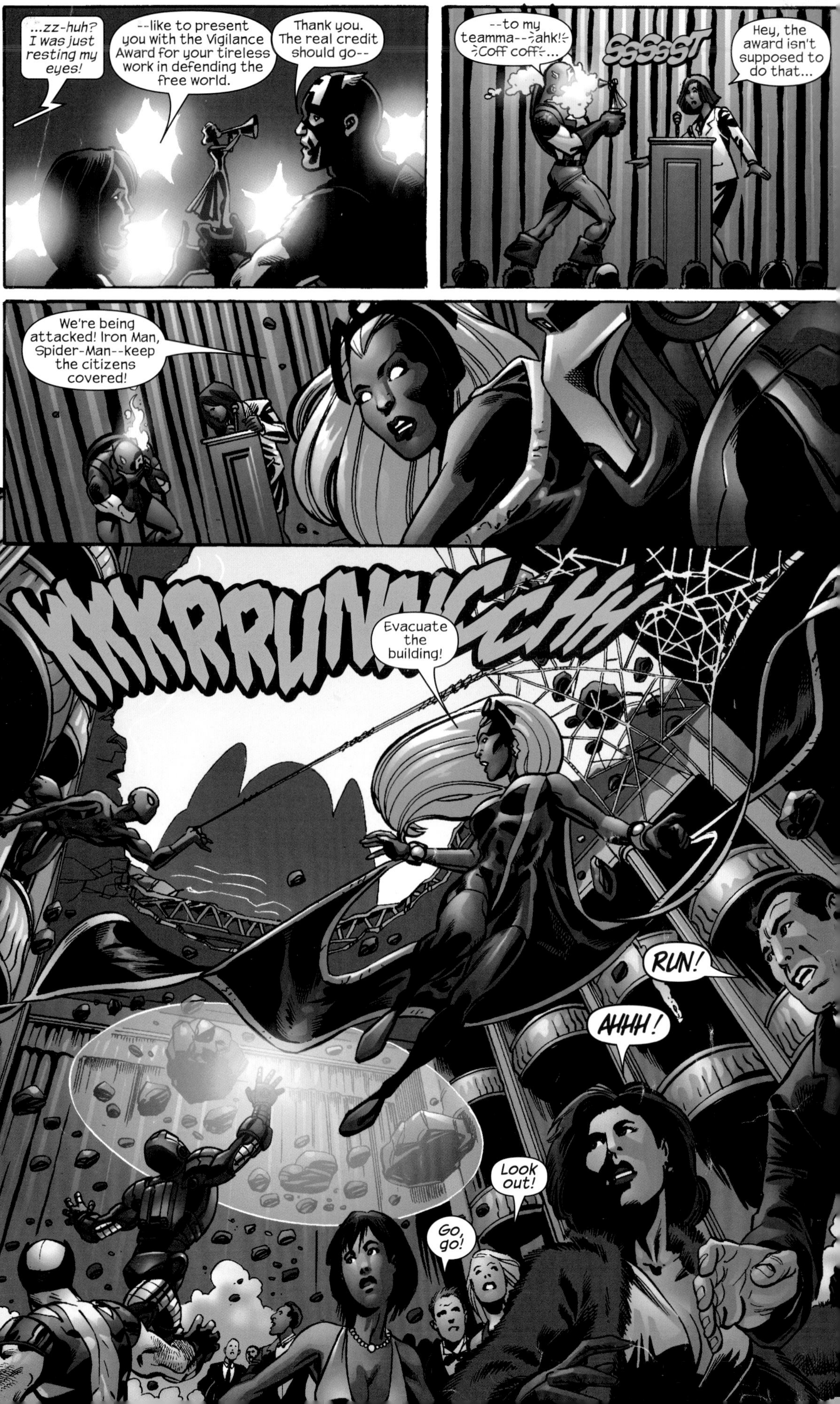

...zz-huh? I was just resting my eyes!
--like to present you with the Vigilance Award for your tireless work in defending the free world.
Thank you. The real credit should go--
--to my teamma--ahk! Coff coff...
SSSSST
Hey, the award isn't supposed to do that...
We're being attacked! Iron Man, Spider-Man--keep the citizens covered!
Evacuate the building!
RUN!
AHHH!
Look out!
Go, go!

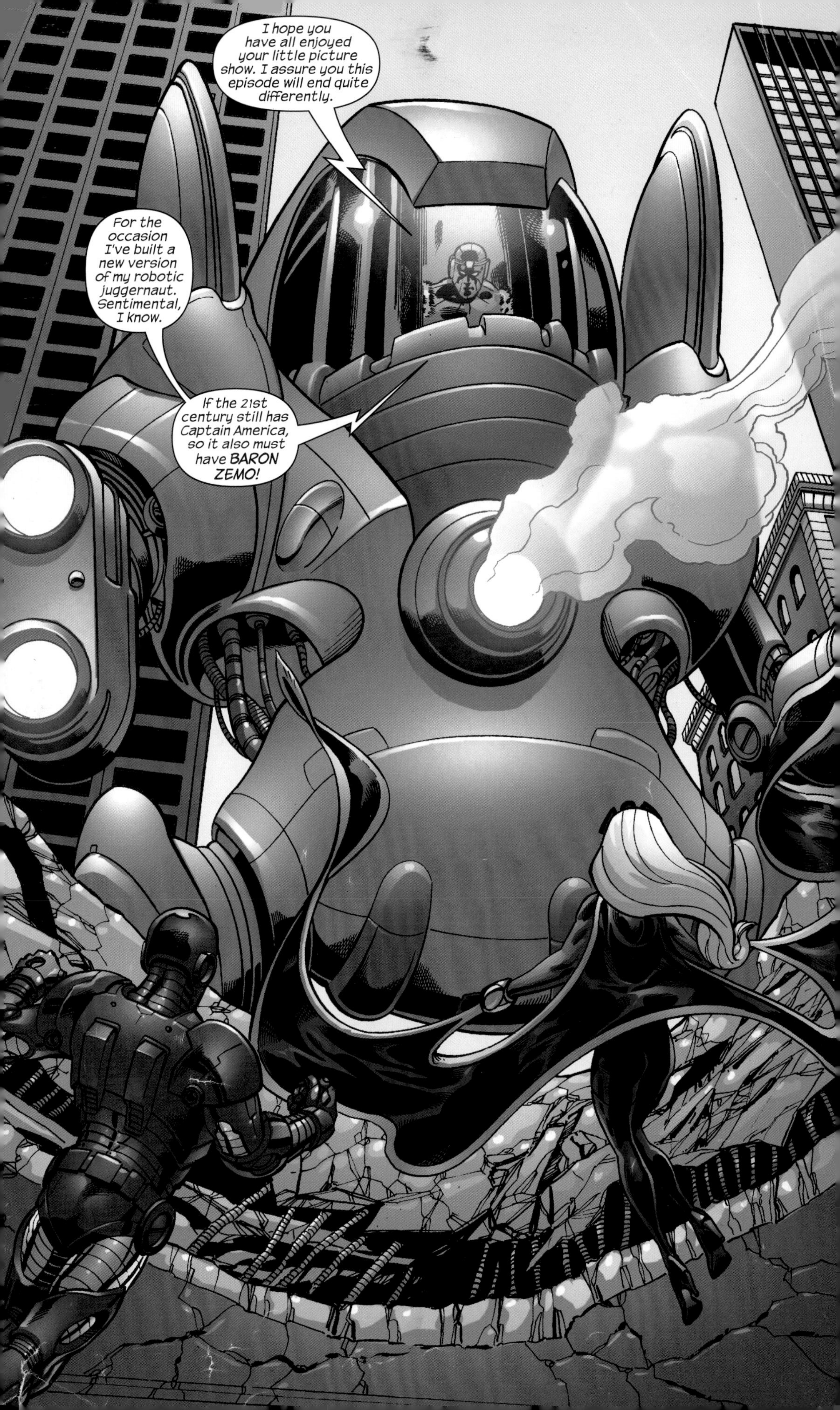

I hope you have all enjoyed your little picture show. I assure you this episode will end quite differently.
For the occasion I've built a new version of my robotic juggernaut. Sentimental, I know.
If the 21st century still has Captain America, so it also must have BARON ZEMO!

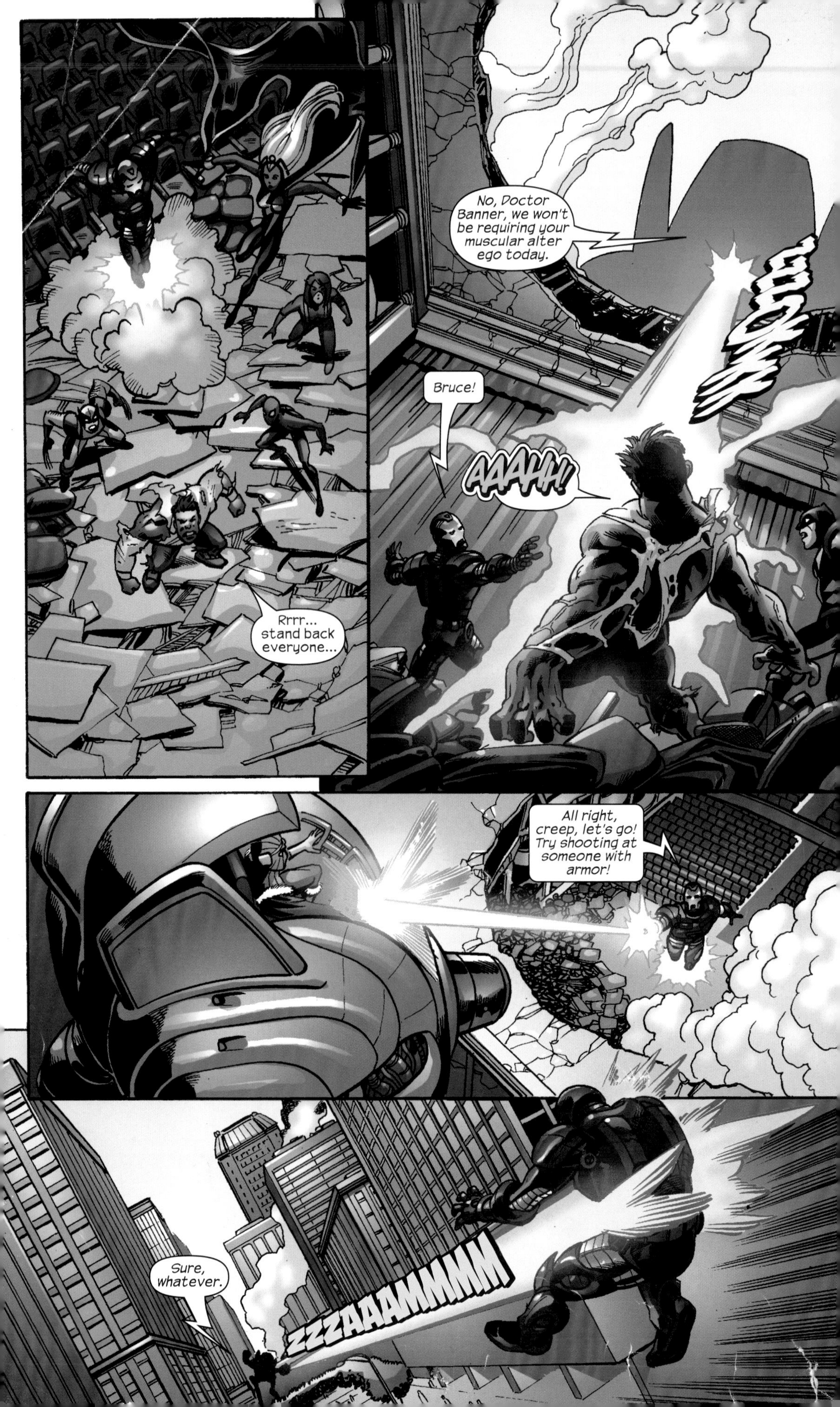

Rrrr... stand back everyone...
No, Doctor Banner, we won't be requiring your muscular alter ego today.
Bruce!
AAAHH!
All right, creep, let's go! Try shooting at someone with armor!
Sure, whatever.
ZZZAAAMMMMM

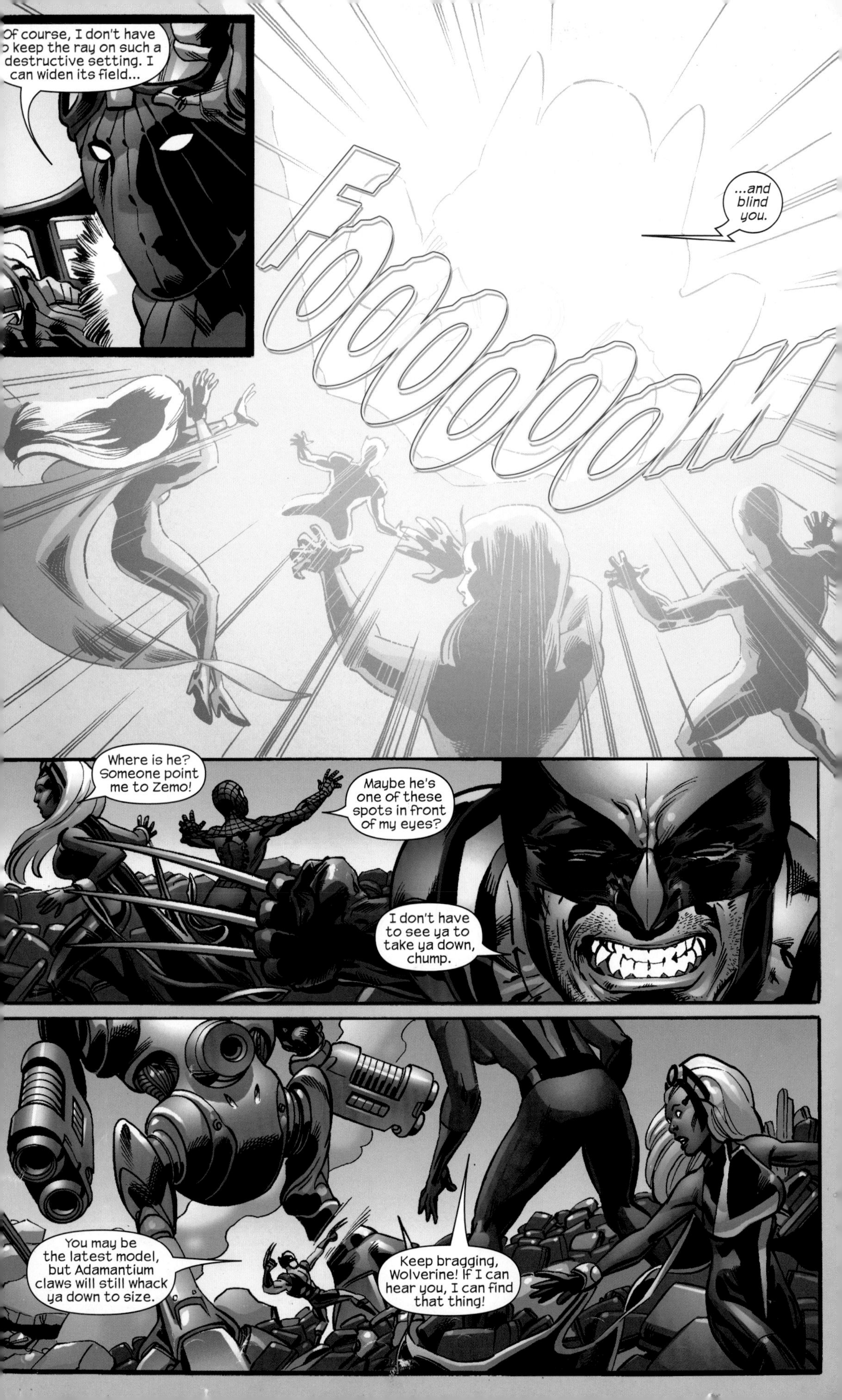
Of course, I don't have to keep the ray on such a destructive setting. I can widen its field...
FOOOOOOOOM
...and blind you.
Where is he? Someone point me to Zemo!
Maybe he's one of these spots in front of my eyes?
I don't have to see ya to take ya down, chump.
You may be the latest model, but Adamantium claws will still whack ya down to size.
Keep bragging, Wolverine! If I can hear you, I can find that thing!

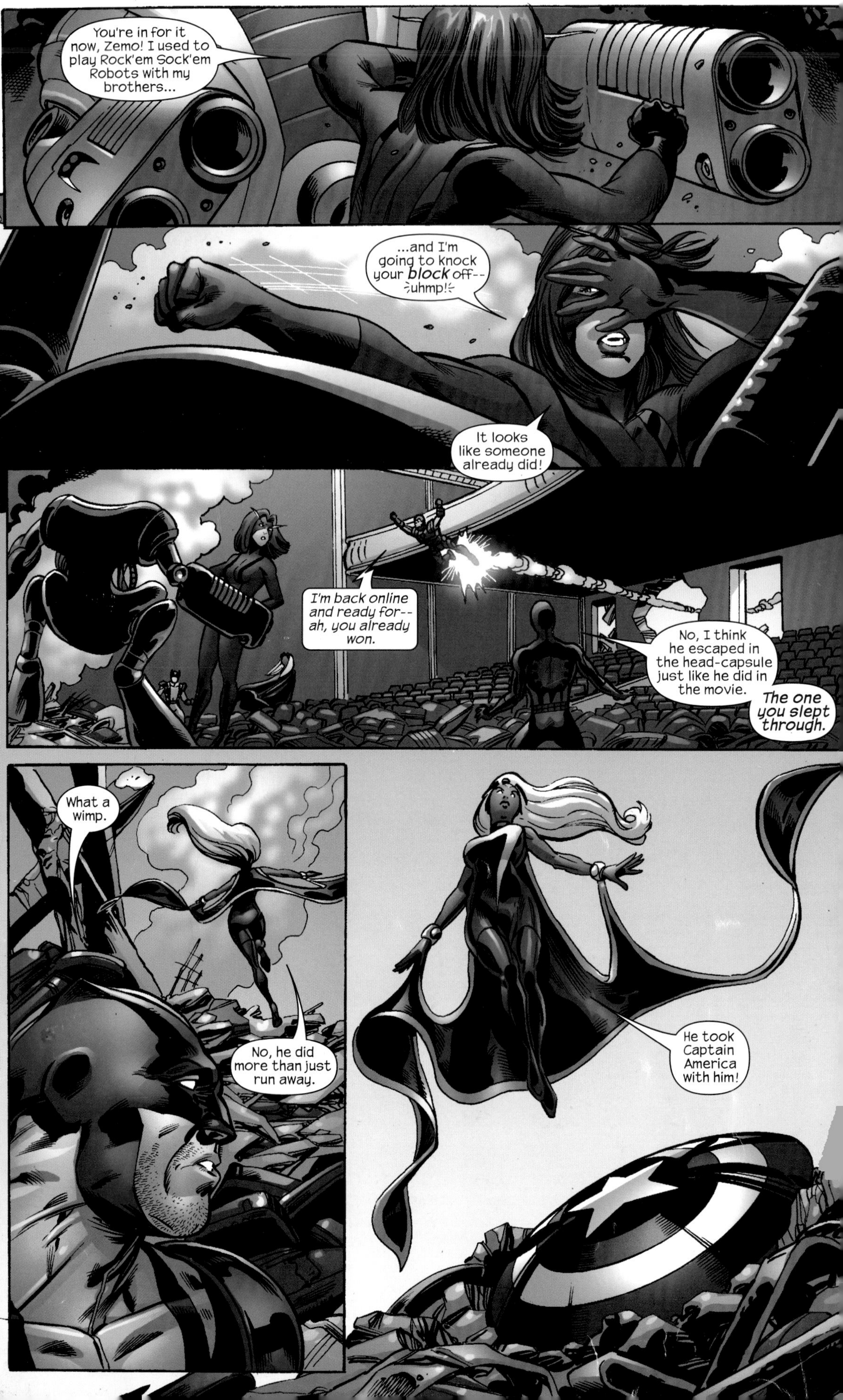

You're in for it now, Zemo! I used to play Rock'em Sock'em Robots with my brothers...
...and I'm going to knock your *block* off-- -uhmp!-
It looks like someone already did!
I'm back online and ready for-- ah, you already won.
No, I think he escaped in the head-capsule just like he did in the movie.
The one you slept through.
What a wimp.
No, he did more than just run away.
He took Captain America with him!

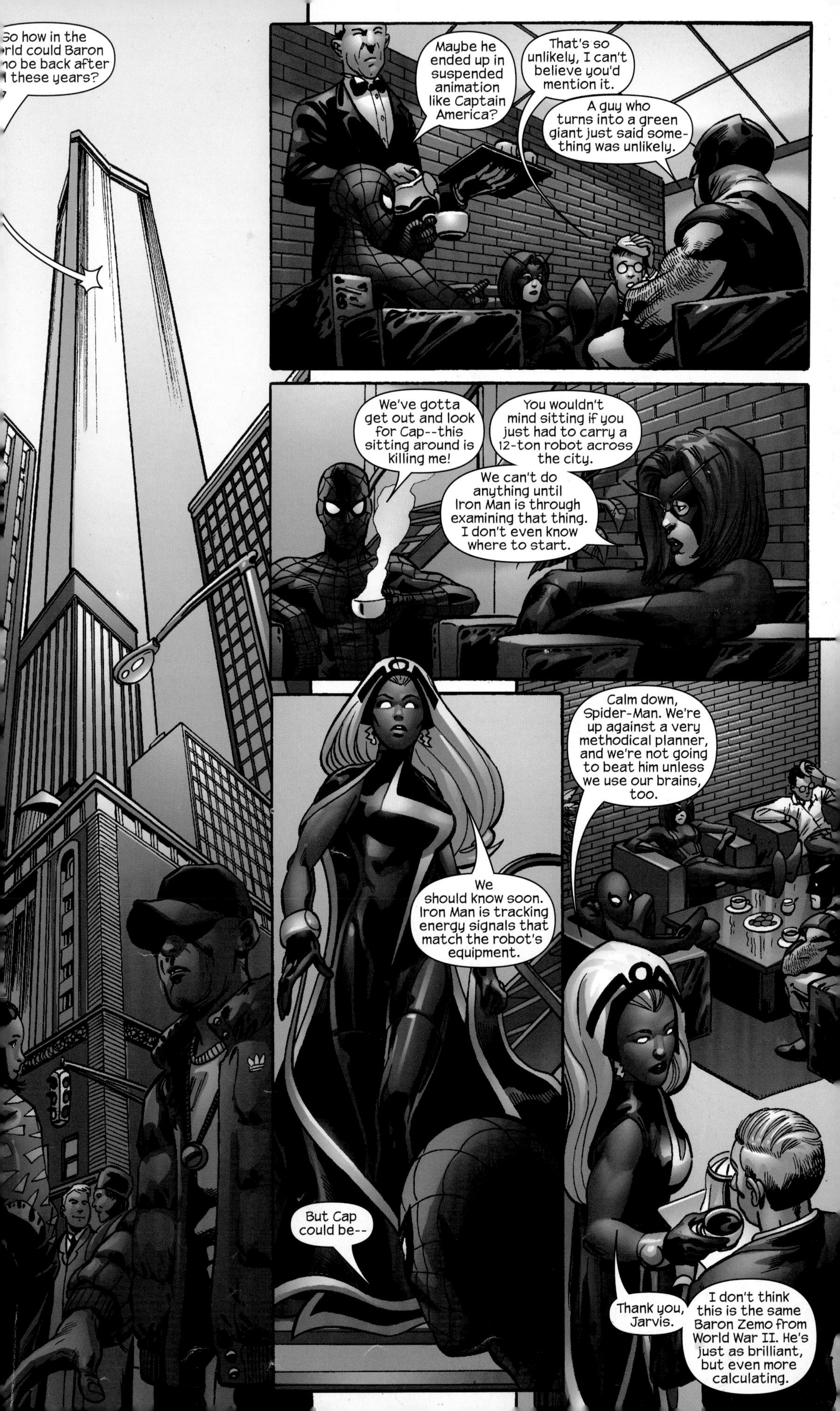
So how in the
rld could Baron
mo be back after
these years?
Maybe he ended up in suspended animation like Captain America?
That's so unlikely, I can't believe you'd mention it.
A guy who turns into a green giant just said something was unlikely.
We've gotta get out and look for Cap--this sitting around is killing me!
You wouldn't mind sitting if you just had to carry a 12-ton robot across the city.
We can't do anything until Iron Man is through examining that thing. I don't even know where to start.
Calm down, Spider-Man. We're up against a very methodical planner, and we're not going to beat him unless we use our brains, too.
We should know soon. Iron Man is tracking energy signals that match the robot's equipment.
But Cap could be--
Thank you, Jarvis.
I don't think this is the same Baron Zemo from World War II. He's just as brilliant, but even more calculating.

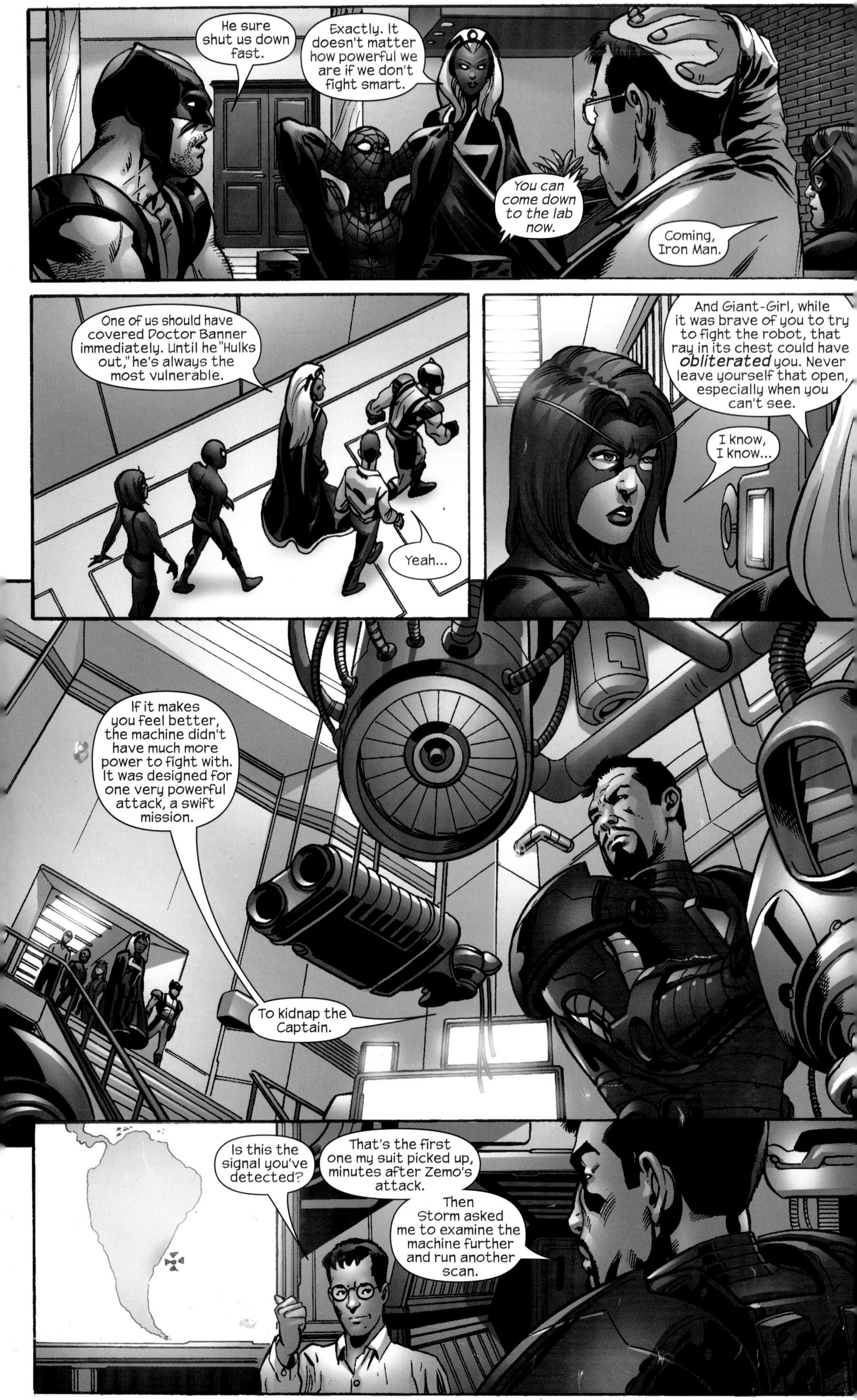
He sure shut us down fast.
Exactly. It doesn't matter how powerful we are if we don't fight smart.
You can come down to the lab now.
Coming, Iron Man.
One of us should have covered Doctor Banner immediately. Until he "Hulks out," he's always the most vulnerable.
Yeah...
And Giant-Girl, while it was brave of you to try to fight the robot, that ray in its chest could have obliterated you. Never leave yourself that open, especially when you can't see.
I know, I know...
If it makes you feel better, the machine didn't have much more power to fight with. It was designed for one very powerful attack, a swift mission.
To kidnap the Captain.
Is this the signal you've detected?
That's the first one my suit picked up, minutes after Zemo's attack.
Then Storm asked me to examine the machine further and run another scan.

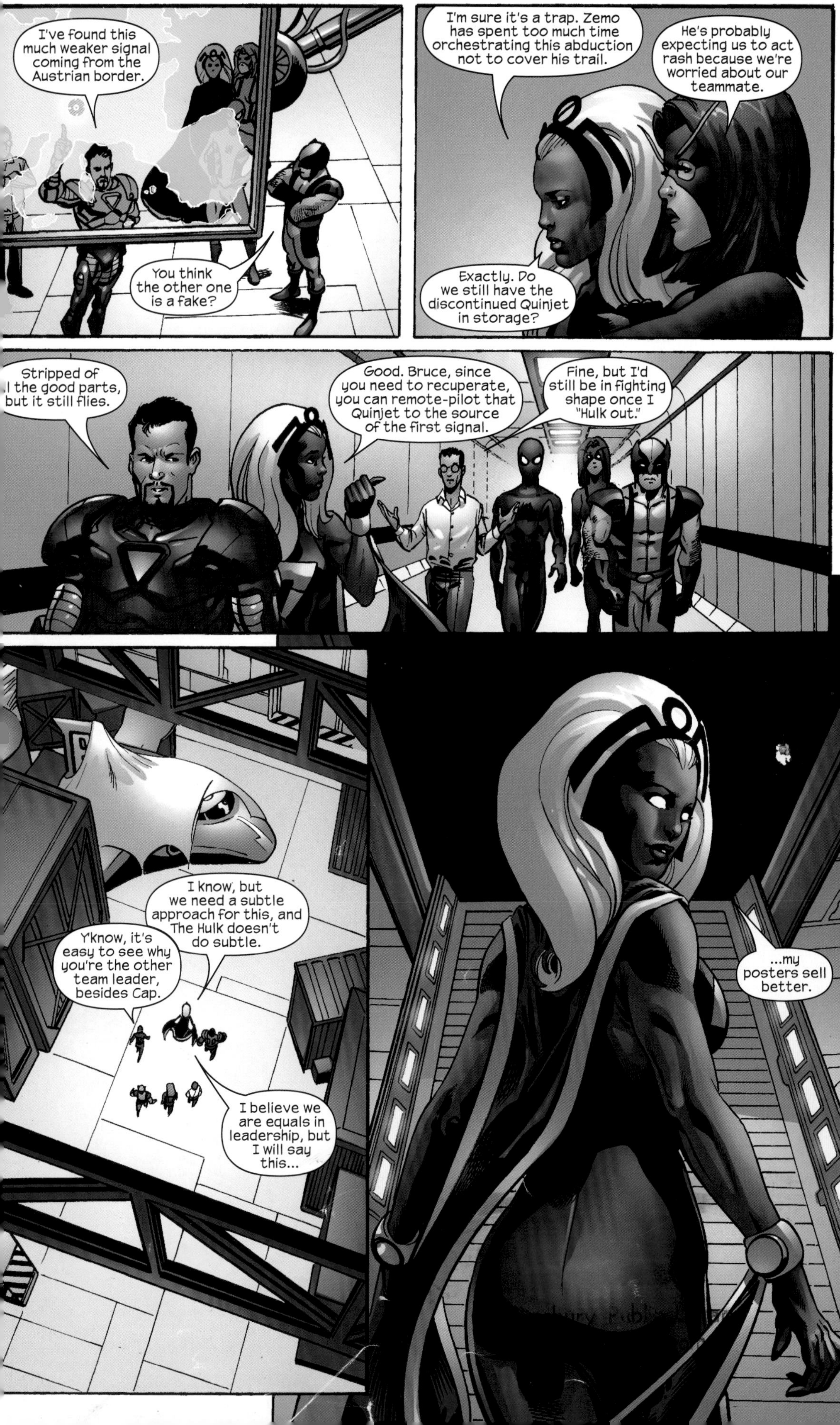

I've found this much weaker signal coming from the Austrian border.
You think the other one is a fake?
I'm sure it's a trap. Zemo has spent too much time orchestrating this abduction not to cover his trail.
He's probably expecting us to act rash because we're worried about our teammate.
Exactly. Do we still have the discontinued Quinjet in storage?
Stripped of l the good parts, but it still flies.
Good. Bruce, since you need to recuperate, you can remote-pilot that Quinjet to the source of the first signal.
Fine, but I'd still be in fighting shape once I "Hulk out."
I know, but we need a subtle approach for this, and The Hulk doesn't do subtle.
Y'know, it's easy to see why you're the other team leader, besides Cap.
I believe we are equals in leadership, but I will say this...
...my posters sell better.

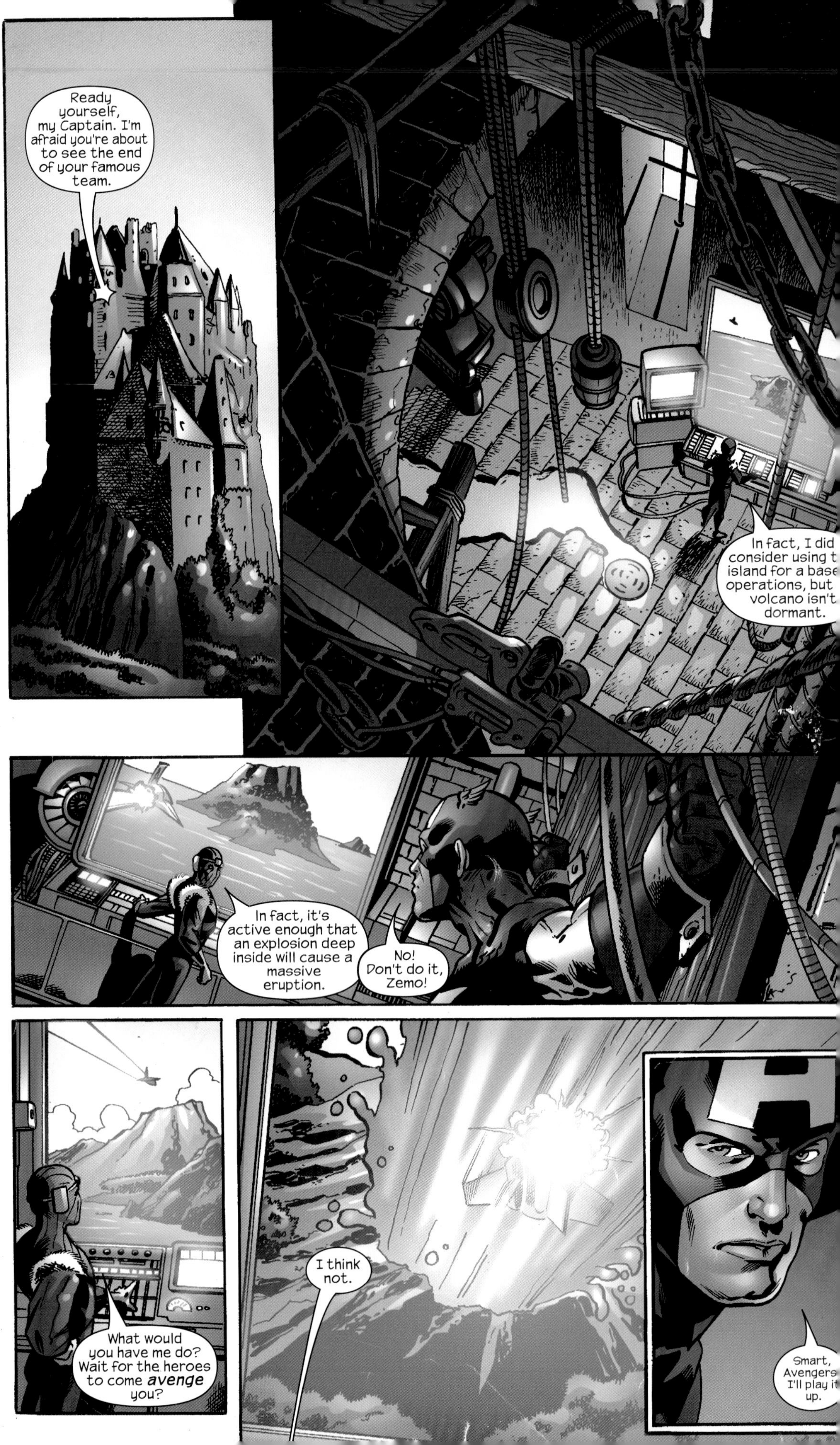

Ready yourself, my Captain. I'm afraid you're about to see the end of your famous team.
In fact, I did consider using t island for a base operations, but volcano isn't dormant.
In fact, it's active enough that an explosion deep inside will cause a massive eruption.
No! Don't do it, Zemo!
What would you have me do? Wait for the heroes to come *avenge* you?
I think not.
Smart, Avengers I'll play it up.

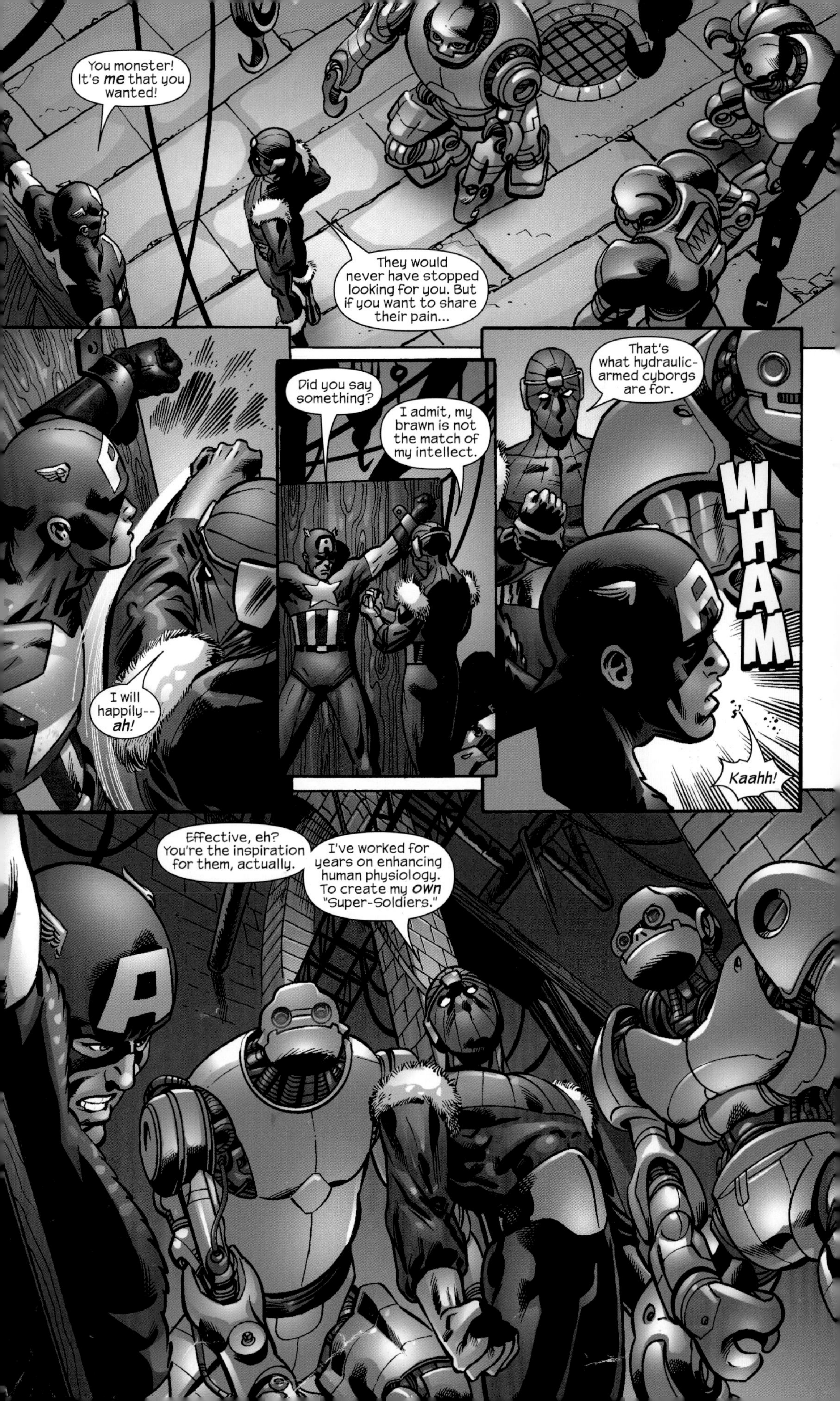
You monster! It's *me* that you wanted!
They would never have stopped looking for you. But if you want to share their pain...
I will happily-- *ah!*
Did you say something?
I admit, my brawn is not the match of my intellect.
That's what hydraulic-armed cyborgs are for.
WHAM
Kaahh!
Effective, eh? You're the inspiration for them, actually.
I've worked for years on enhancing human physiology. To create my *OWN* "Super-Soldiers."

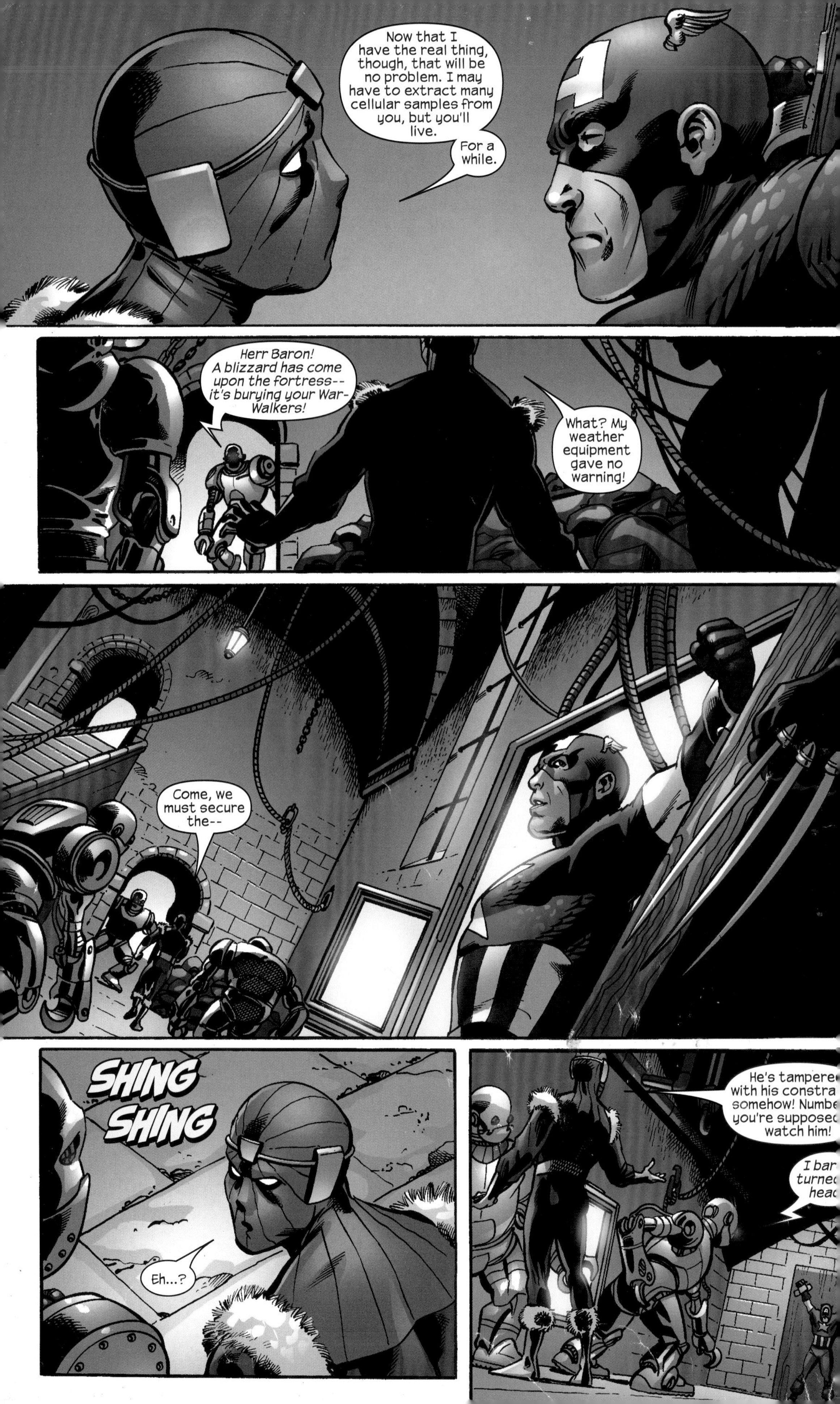
Now that I have the real thing, though, that will be no problem. I may have to extract many cellular samples from you, but you'll live.
For a while.
Herr Baron! A blizzard has come upon the fortress--it's burying your War-Walkers!
What? My weather equipment gave no warning!
Come, we must secure the--
SHING SHING
Eh...?
He's tampere with his constra somehow! Numbe you're supposec watch him!
I bar turnec heac

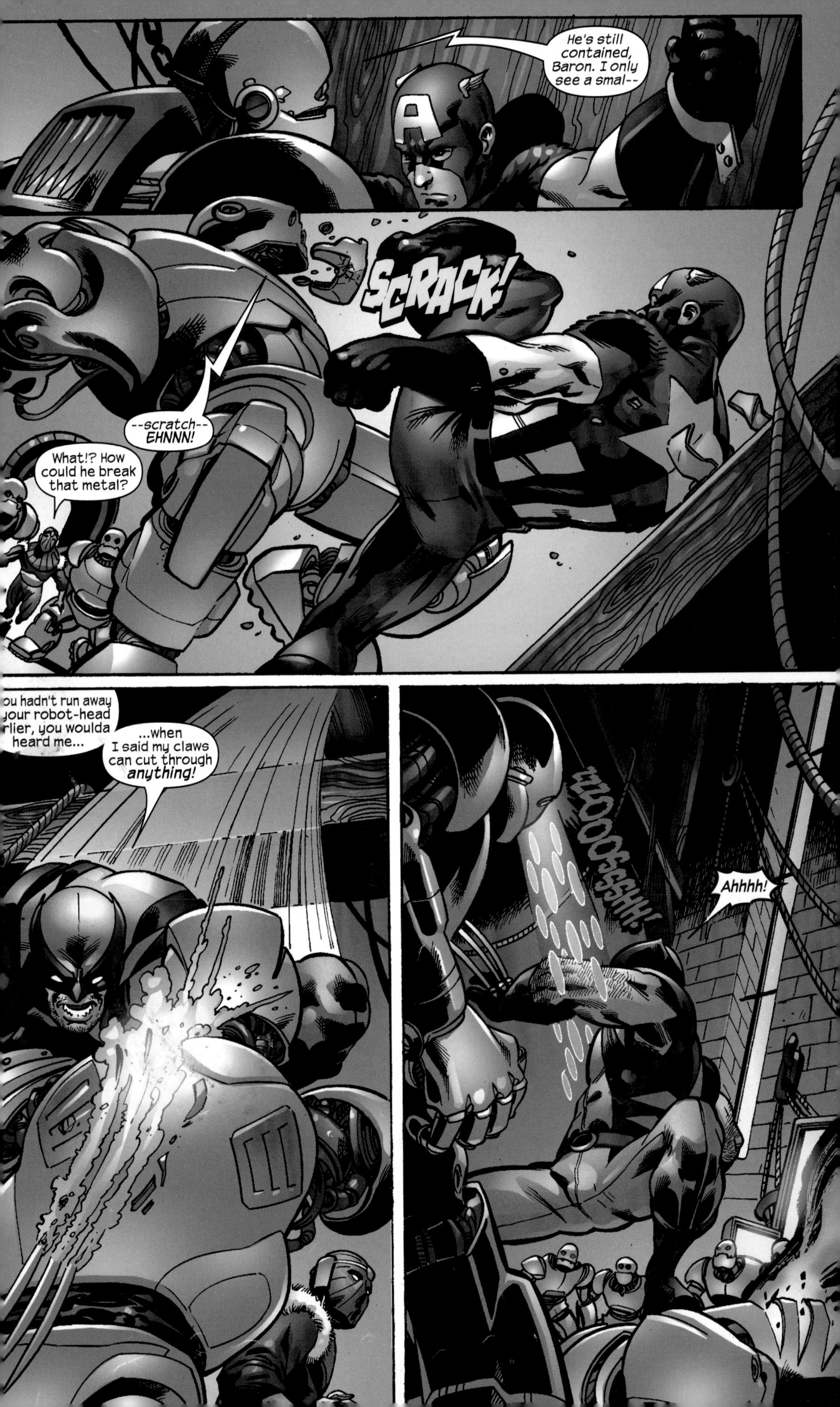
He's still contained, Baron. I only see a smal--
SCRACK!
--scratch-- EHNNN!
What!? How could he break that metal?
ou hadn't run away your robot-head rlier, you woulda heard me...
...when I said my claws can cut through *anything!*
ZZZOOOSSSHH!
Ahhhh!

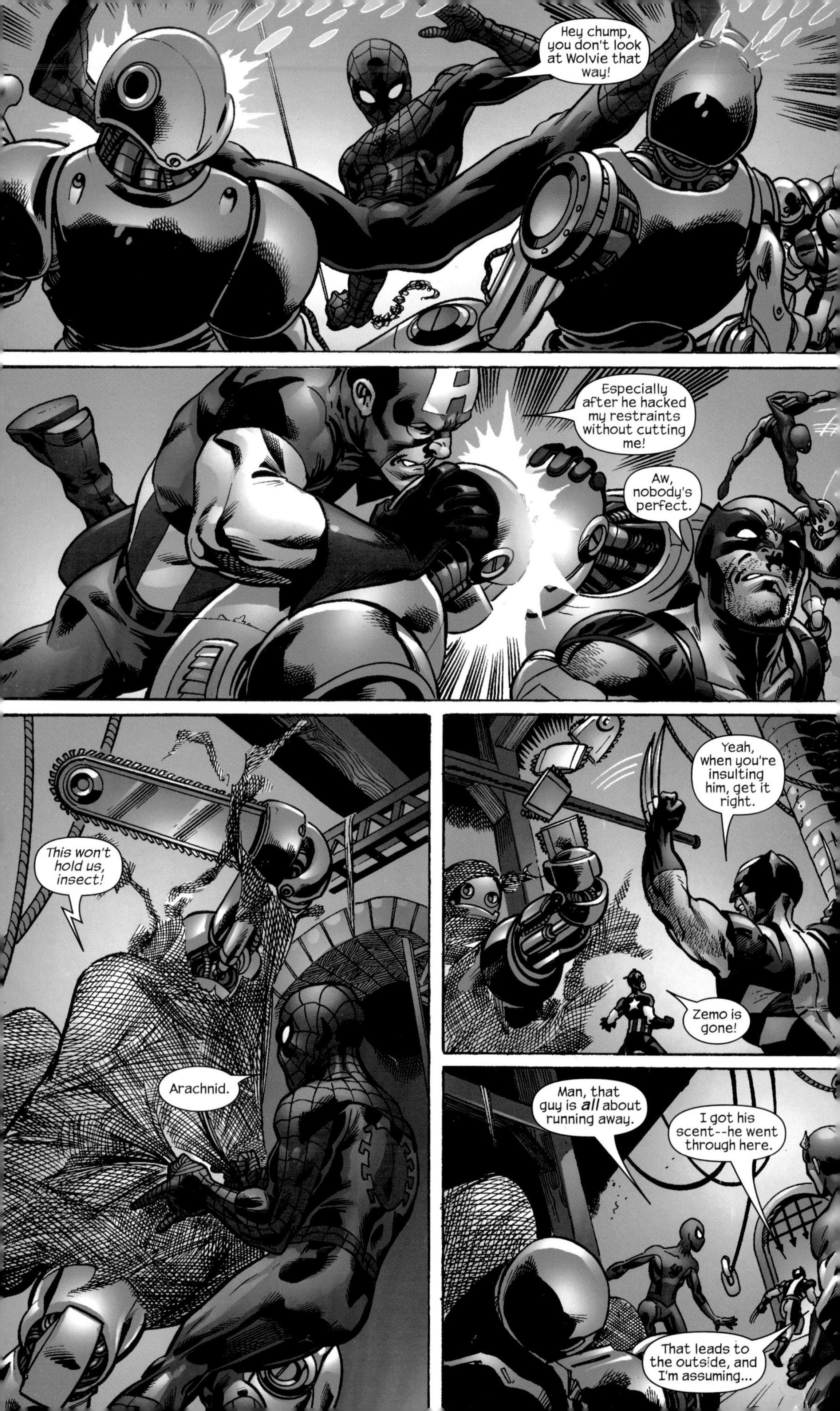
Hey chump, you don't look at Wolvie that way!
Especially after he hacked my restraints without cutting me!
Aw, nobody's perfect.
This won't hold us, insect!
Arachnid.
Yeah, when you're insulting him, get it right.
Zemo is gone!
Man, that guy is *all* about running away.
I got his scent--he went through here.
That leads to the outside, and I'm assuming...

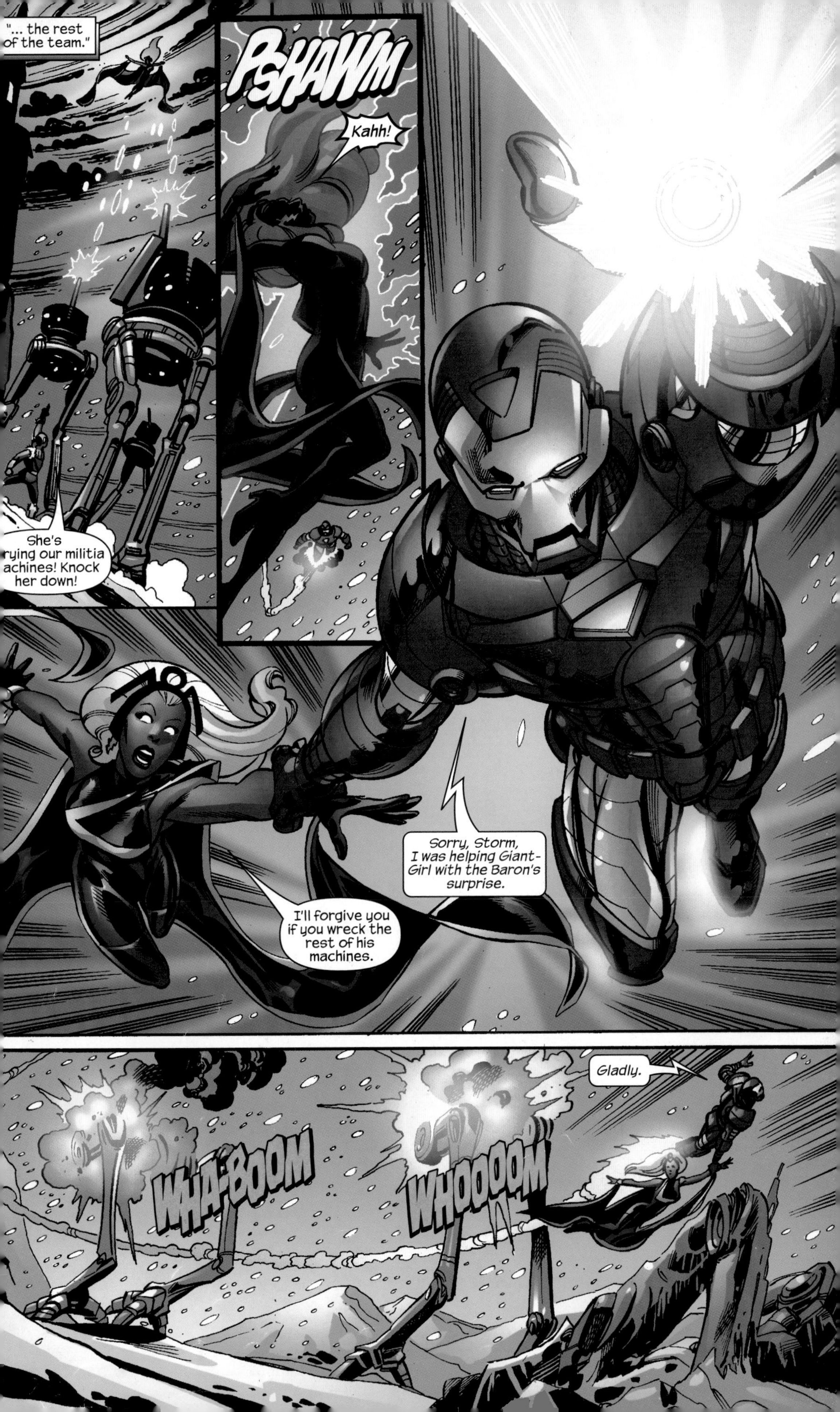
"... the rest of the team."
PSHAWM
Kahh!
She's rying our militia achines! Knock her down!
Sorry, Storm, I was helping Giant-Girl with the Baron's surprise.
I'll forgive you if you wreck the rest of his machines.
Gladly.
WHA-BOOM
WHOOOOM

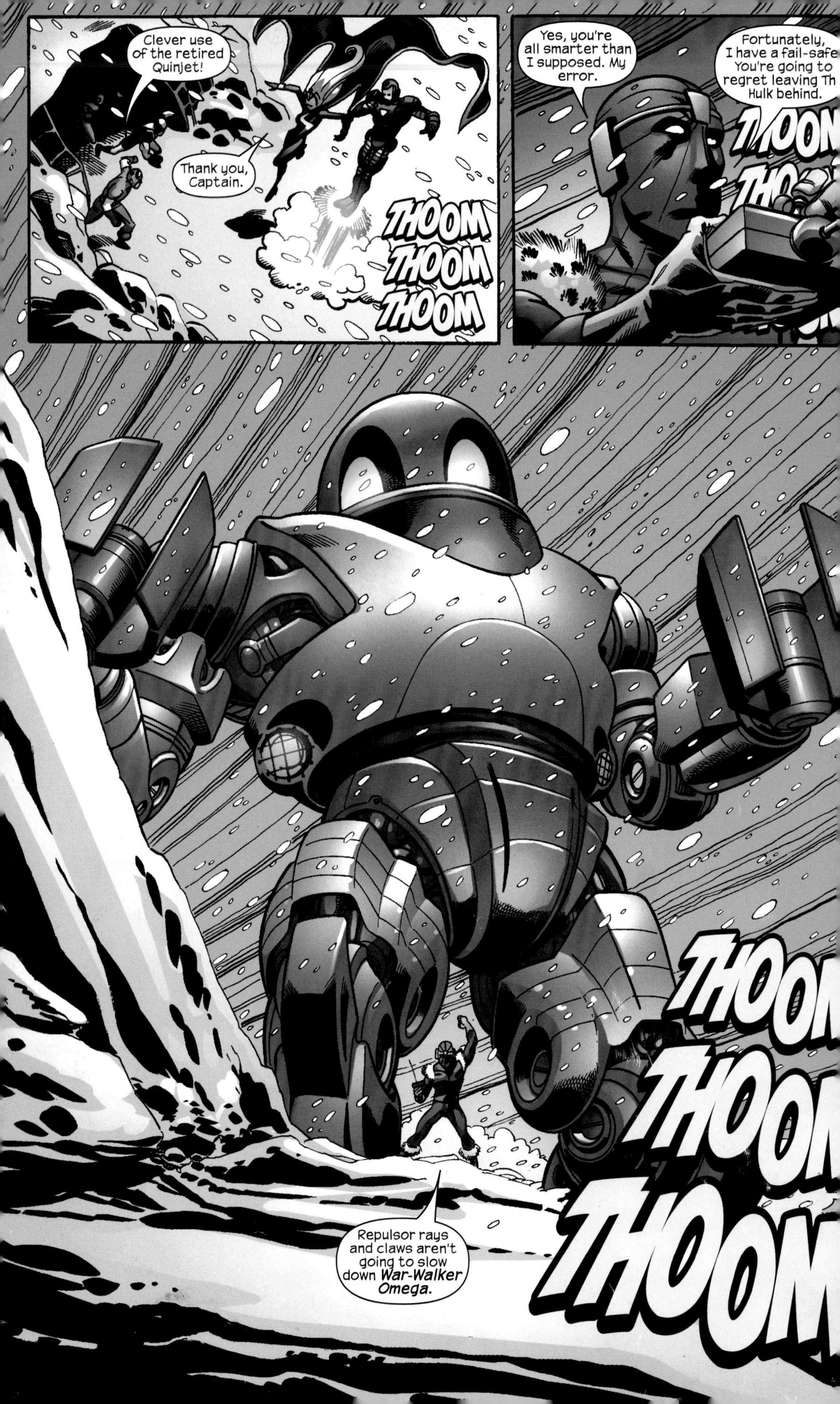

Clever use of the retired Quinjet!
Thank you, Captain.
THOOM THOOM THOOM
Yes, you're all smarter than I supposed. My error.
Fortunately, I have a fail-safe. You're going to regret leaving The Hulk behind.
THOOM THOOM
THOOM THOOM THOOM
Repulsor rays and claws aren't going to slow down *War-Walker Omega.*

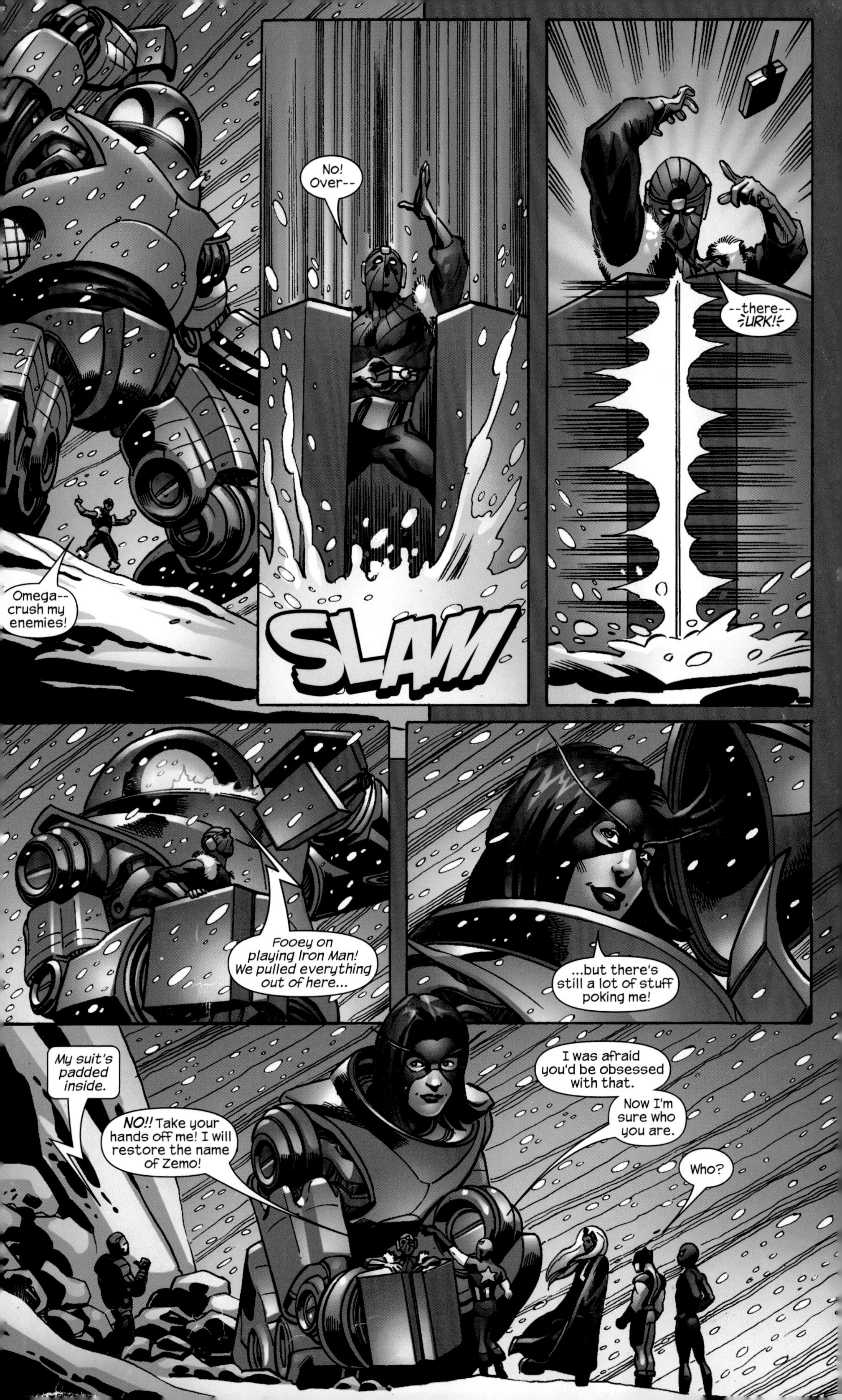
Omega--
crush my
enemies!
No!
Over--
SLAM
--there--
URK!
Fooey on playing Iron Man! We pulled everything out of here...
...but there's still a lot of stuff poking me!
My suit's padded inside.
NO!! Take your hands off me! I will restore the name of Zemo!
I was afraid you'd be obsessed with that.
Now I'm sure who you are.
Who?

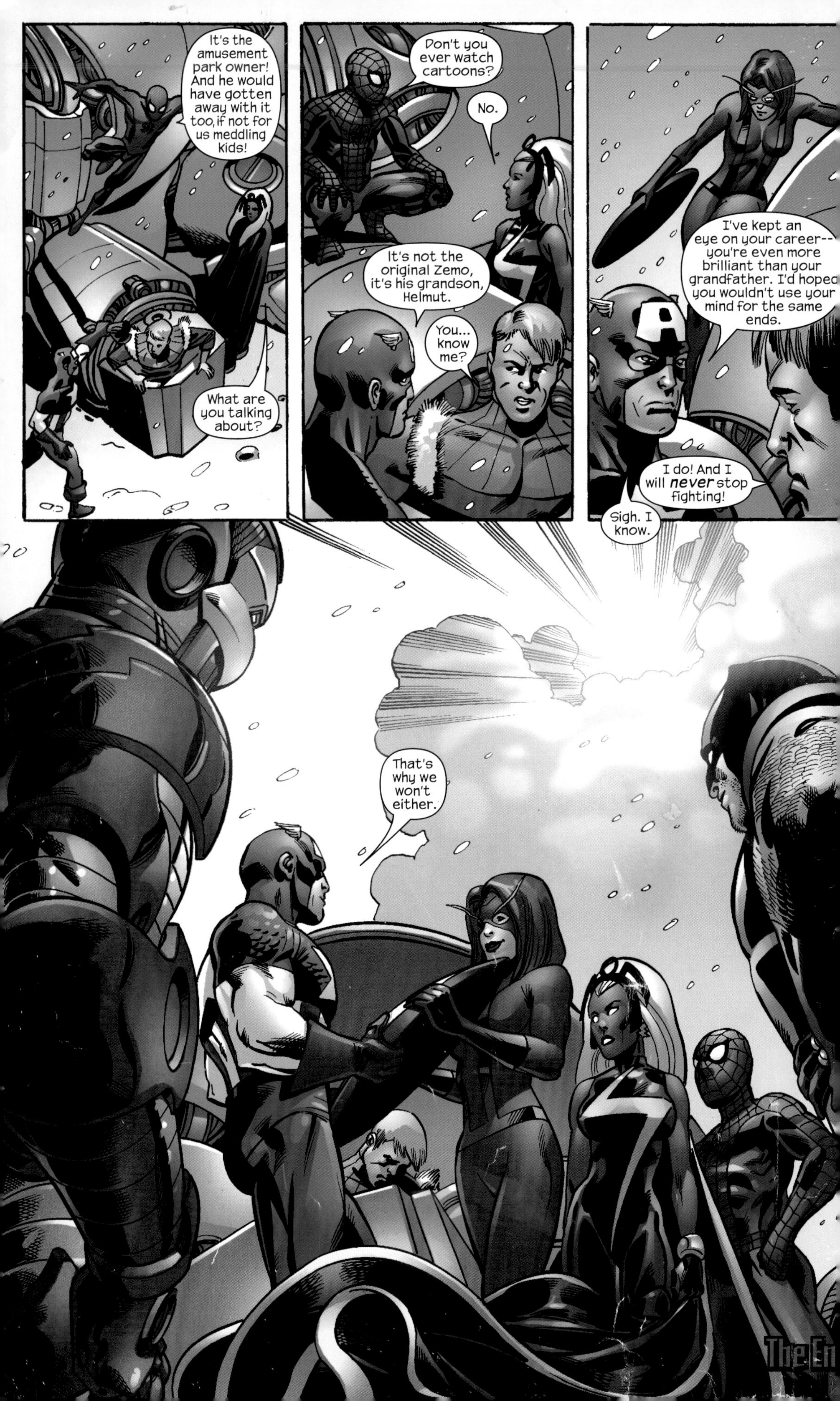
It's the amusement park owner! And he would have gotten away with it too, if not for us meddling kids!
What are you talking about?
Don't you ever watch cartoons?
No.
It's not the original Zemo, it's his grandson, Helmut.
You... know me?
I've kept an eye on your career--you're even more brilliant than your grandfather. I'd hoped you wouldn't use your mind for the same ends.
I do! And I will never stop fighting!
Sigh. I know.
That's why we won't either.
The En

Simsbury Public Library
Children's Room
725 Hopmeadow Street
Simsbury, CT 06070